Little, Brown and Company

Hachette Book Group
1290 Avenue of the Americas, New York, NY 10104
Visit us at lb-kids.com
mylittlepony.com

LB kids is an imprint of Little, Brown and Company.
The LB kids name and logo are trademarks of Hachette Book Group, Inc.

The publisher is not responsible for websites (or their content) that are not owned by the publisher.

First Edition: January 2015

Library of Congress Cataloging-in-Publication Data

Alexander, Louise (Louise Shirreffs), 1979–
Hooray for spring! / by Louise Alexander. — First edition.
   pages cm. — (My little pony)
   ISBN 978-0-316-40542-3 (pbk)
   I. Title.
   PZ7.A37746Hoo 2015
   [E]—dc23
                                    2013046475

10 9 8 7 6 5 4 3 2 1

CW

Printed in the United States of America

HOORAY FOR SPRING!

Based on the episode by **Cindy Morrow**
Adapted by **Louise Alexander**

LITTLE, BROWN & COMPANY
LB kids

Twilight Sparkle leaped out of bed. "Hooray for spring!"

After months of cold temperatures and snow, it was finally time for Ponyville's Winter Wrap-Up!

Spike rolled over groggily. "Nooooo, let me keep hibernating," he said, pulling the covers over his head.

"Come on, Spike! Winter Wrap-Up is an annual tradition! I'm so excited to prepare Ponyville for sunshine and rainbows and flowers and animals!"

Twilight gleefully checked off the items she needed for a hard day of work.

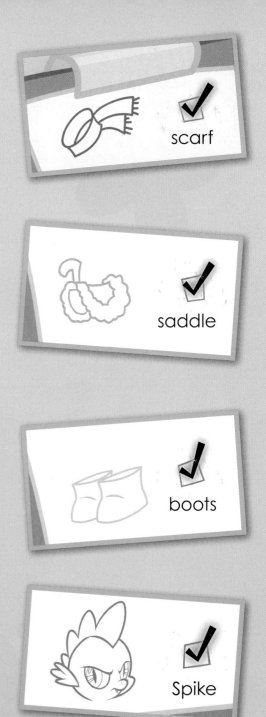

scarf

saddle

boots

Spike

Twilight finally roused Spike from his sleep, and they arrived at Town Hall just as the mayor of Ponyville called everypony to join Spring Awakening.

"I need you to share your talents! We have a lot of work to do by the end of the day! You've each been assigned a team," said the mayor. "Weather team, your leader is Rainbow Dash!"

"Flight crew, let's clear out these clouds and bring sunshine back to Ponyville!" called out Rainbow Dash. "I'm also gonna need a group to guide birds back from the south."

A team of Pegasi gathered, eager to take off into the skies. Twilight looked at them with envy, wishing she was a natural flyer. Alas, she had no wings!

"Pinkie Pie needs help on the ground...
er, ice," the mayor went on.

"Wheeeeeeeeeeeeeeee!" Pinkie Pie
slid by on a pair of ice skates.

"Ice crew, you slice the ice so when
the sun comes out, it breaks up nice and
neat," said the mayor.

Twilight looked nervously at the frozen
lake. She had never been on ice skates
before and didn't see a good reason to
start a new sport *now*!

"Plant team, report to Applejack!" called the mayor.

"Okay, y'all," Applejack said. "We've got a lot of hard work ahead. I need the strongest ponies to pull plows and clear snow out of the fields!"

Big McIntosh and his friends stepped forward. "Eeyup."

"Great, Big Mac! Y'all will need a posse to plant seeds once the snow's gone. There are a lot of crops to grow!"

Twilight sighed. No way was she strong enough to drive a plow.

She didn't know what she'd be able to do without her magic, which wasn't allowed.

"Last but not least, the animal team follows Fluttershy," the mayor finished.

Fluttershy stepped up to the microphone bashfully. "Wake up our cute little friends from their long winter sleep, but be kind and gentle as we visit their homes."

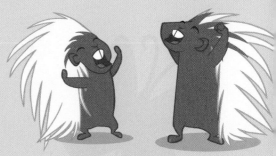

Fluttershy continued. "Some of you will build nests with Rarity to welcome our feathered friends from the south."

Rarity held up a perfectly rounded bowl made of sticks and hay woven together with bright, shiny ribbons.

Spike whistled. "That's some fancy real estate for an egg!"

The mayor blew a whistle. "All right, ponies! Go awaken spring!" As everypony followed their leaders, Twilight sighed.

"C'mon, Spike, we'll just have to see who needs us the most."

Fluttershy's team had the kindest and craftiest ponies. While Fluttershy gently called into every den to wake up sleeping critters, Rarity lovingly constructed elaborate nests.

Twilight noted they seemed to be moving a little too slow. There were still hundreds of nests to build and dozens more critters to awaken!

There was no doubt Rainbow Dash's team had the fastest flyers. But Twilight noticed there were still an awful lot of clouds in the sky. Without more sun, it would take forever to clear the snow.

Sure enough, even though Applejack's team had the strongest ponies, mounds of snow still covered the fields.

Twilight felt sad that she hadn't helped her friends. Plus, it seemed impossible that the ponies would be finished readying Ponyville to welcome spring before sunset.

As she stood thinking of the best way to help, the team leaders started arguing.

"Weather team, move those clouds faster," yelled Applejack. "I need more sun to melt that darn snow!"

"Simmer down, AJ," snapped Rainbow. "I can't work my team any faster. They're exhausted!"

"If anything, we should move *slower,*" Fluttershy warned. "If we startle the animals, we'll scare them back into hibernation."

Twilight suddenly had a great idea. She whispered for Spike to fetch her clipboard.

"What is this fighting about?" the mayor demanded.

Applejack, Rainbow, and Fluttershy looked down, embarrassed.

"No problem here!" Twilight interrupted. "We were just reviewing the final checklists. AHEM, RIGHT, ponies?"

Twilight's friends nodded and turned to her for instructions.

"Ponies, it's time to do what I do best: Get organized!"

The ponies groaned.

"I know it might not sound fun to you, but making to-do lists and checking things off is *my* special talent. If we work together, I just know we can finish Winter Wrap-Up on time!"

For the next few hours, the ponies raced to finish their tasks. They formed an assembly line to build nests, skated in precise lines to cut the ice into a neat grid, and strung bells across the animal dens to wake them all up with a gentle alarm.

Just before sundown, the mayor called Twilight onstage.
"Before I pronounce the official arrival of spring, I want to thank Twilight Sparkle for helping everyone work together. From now on, she will be Winter Wrap-Up's All-Team Organizer!" Twilight put on a special vest.

Twilight blushed. "I couldn't have done it without my friends. Everypony worked so hard today!"

Suddenly, thousands of colorful birds filled the sky, trees blossomed with fragrant pink flowers, and bright rays of sunlight sparkled off the surface of the lake.

"Hooray for spring!" Twilight whooped.

"Hooray!" the ponies cheered. Twilight and her friends could not remember Ponyville ever looking so pretty.

Just when Twilight didn't think the day could be more beautiful, Rainbow Dash launched upward and produced a beautiful rainbow. Everypony looked in awe as it stretched across the sky.

"What a magical way to start spring." Twilight smiled.

Spike nodded in agreement. Then he curled up for a nap in a perfect puddle of sunshine.